Hello Kitty
The Nutcracker

HarperCollins *Children's Books*

Hello Kitty is...
Clara

Dear Daniel is...
the Nutcracker Prince

Thomas is...
Uncle Toymaker

Tippy is...
Cousin Henry

Hello Kitty
The Nutcracker

© 1976, 2014 SANRIO CO., LTD
First published in the UK by HarperCollins *Children's Books* in 2014
1 3 5 7 9 10 8 6 4 2
ISBN: 978-0-00-755944-2

Written by Stella Gurney
Designed by Anna Lubecka

www.harpercollins.co.uk

Printed and bound in China

Cast

Mimmy is...

the Sugar Plum Fairy

Fifi is...

a party guest

Timmy is...

a naughty mouse

Tammy is...

another naughty mouse!

Hello Kitty and her friends are very excited. They are putting on a special play for their families.

Dusk is falling outside and the air is chilly. Here in the school hall, it's warm and cosy as the audience take their seats for...

The Nutcracker!

Once upon a time, there was a young girl called Clara. Her family lived in a big house in an old city, and tonight they were having a party to celebrate Christmas Eve.

Clara was decorating the tree. Carefully, she hung the shiny baubles, the brightly wrapped sweets and candy canes and the little painted wooden figures. At the top, she placed a beautiful new fairy with a sparkling tiara and skirts the colour of sugar plums.

Ding Dong

The guests started to arrive and the party began.
Clara looked out with excitement for her favourite
Uncle, who always brought her beautiful gifts.

Tonight he had made her a wonderful painted wooden nutcracker, with arms and legs that moved!

"Thank you, Uncle," smiled the little girl, and she ran off to play with it.

But alas, during the evening, Clara's cousin Henry stepped on the nutcracker by accident, breaking its leg.

"Sorry, Clara," said Cousin Henry.

"Don't worry," said Uncle kindly as Clara wept. "I can mend it for you."

He carefully put the toy back together, and then whispered a few words in its ear.

"There," smiled Uncle. "Now he's fixed."

After everyone had left and the house was sleeping, two naughty mice came out to play. They saw the nutcracker lying on the floor. "Let's hide it, tee hee!" they giggled.

Upstairs, Clara awoke
suddenly to hear the clock
chiming midnight. She remembered
she had left her nutcracker downstairs
and hurried down to look for it.

Something magical had happened! The stairs led down to
a forest floor, covered in pine needles. Trees stood where the
walls of her home had been, and a full moon shone in the sky.
Clara looked round in astonishment. Suddenly a sweet voice
commanded, "Mice – return Clara's nutcracker".

Two mice came meekly from behind a tree,
one of them holding the nutcracker toy.

To Clara's amazement, the nutcracker smiled. Then, in one magical movement, it began to grow until it was the same size as Clara. There before her, stood a handsome Nutcracker Prince!

"Whatever has happened?" gasped Clara. "It's the Sugar Plum Fairy's magic," smiled the Nutcracker Prince.

Clara looked up in wonder.

"It's true," laughed the beautiful Sugar Plum
Fairy, fluttering down from the top of the tree.
"Come with me and I will show you more."

The air around them grew cold, and Clara found herself
holding the Nutcracker Prince's hand, flying over
snowy lands of glittering ice and seas
that sparkled in the moonlight.

Before long, they saw a wonderful castle in the distance, built entirely of sweets and perched on an island of rainbow-coloured sherbet.

The Sugar Plum Fairy ushered them into an enormous sparkling hall. There, dancing to a teddy bear band, were Clara's friends and family, as well as the decorations from her Christmas tree and many of her favourite toys, grown as large as life.

"May I have the pleasure of a dance?" asked the Nutcracker Prince bowing deeply to Clara. "Certainly," laughed Clara, and together they whirled around the glittering hall, happy and breathless.

Next came a magnificent feast. Clara and the Nutcracker
Prince were seated on thrones and the Sugar Plum Fairy
performed a special dance just for them.

It was truly magical. Clara thought this was the most perfect evening ever.

All too soon it was time to go home. Tucked into a sleigh made of sweets and sugared icing, Clara and the Prince waved goodbye. The sleigh took off into the air and Clara leaned drowsily on the shoulder of the Nutcracker Prince.

"I wish the magic would go on forever,"
she murmured, sleepily.

"It can, for those who can see it,"
smiled the Nutcracker Prince.

The next morning, Clara woke in her own warm, cosy bed. Outside, the church bells were ringing for Christmas morning and the smell of gingerbread cookies drifted up from the kitchen.

She gazed at the little wooden nutcracker in her arms.
Was it, could it *really* all have been a dream?

The End

Bravo!

Hooray!

Cheers echo around the hall as the audience claps and shouts for more. Everyone loved the play! Hello Kitty receives a beautiful bouquet of flowers.

Encore!

Hooray!

"I'm glad *this* isn't a dream" she thought. "It's too much fun!" And she took another bow.

Bravo!

The world of

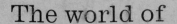

Hello Kitty

Enjoy all of these wonderful Hello Kitty books.

Picture books

Occasion books

Where's Hello Kitty?

 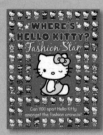 

Activity books

...and more!

Hello Kitty and friends story book series

...and more!